D1029789

Always Tell the Truth

Kyra Robinson

Illustrated by
Cynthia Meadows

BROWN BOOKS KIDS

© 2021 Kyra Robinson

All rights reserved. No part of this book may be used or reproduced in any manner without written permission except in the case of brief quotations embodied in critical articles or reviews.

This is a work of fiction. Any similarity to real persons, living or dead, is coincidental and not intended by the author.

Always Tell the Truth

Brown Books Kids
Dallas / New York
www.BrownBooksKids.com
(972) 381-0009

A New Era in Publishing®

Publisher's Cataloging-In-Publication Data

Names: Robinson, Kyra, author. | Meadows, Cynthia, illustrator.
Title: Always tell the truth / Kyra Robinson ; illustrated by Cynthia Meadows.
Description: Dallas ; New York : Brown Books Kids, [2021] | Interest age level: 005-008. | Summary: "Twins Katie and Kimmie know how important it is to love their neighbors, and one way their Pastor Jimmy says they can do this is to always tell the truth. But when Katie hits a baseball through the Mumfords' kitchen window, she learns that telling the truth is sometimes the hardest thing to do"-- Provided by publisher.
Identifiers: ISBN 9781612545356 (hardcover)
Subjects: LCSH: Twins--Juvenile fiction. | Neighbors--Juvenile fiction. | Honesty--Juvenile fiction. | Truthfulness and falsehood--Juvenile fiction. | CYAC: Twins--Fiction. | Neighbors--Fiction. | Honesty--Fiction.
Classification: LCC PZ7.1.R6366 Al 2021 | DDC [Fic]--dc23

This book has been officially leveled by using the F&P Text Level Gradient™ Leveling System.

ISBN 978-1-61254-535-6
LCCN 2021908789

Printed in the United States
10 9 8 7 6 5 4 3 2 1

For more information or to contact the author, please go to www.BrownBooks.com.

Dedication

To my girls, Kayden and Kiersten, who inspired me to write this book, and to my son, Kelton, who pushes me to be great at whatever I do. I'm extremely proud of you. Everything I do, I do for you three. You guys keep me motivated to be what I am today.

To my childhood neighbors, the late Mr. Alex and Mrs. Mary Shaw, whom my sister and I called grandparents, for showering us with love and kindness every day and showing us what it truly meant to have friends of the family treat you as if you were family. I miss and love you both.

And to my readers, in the hopes that they will remember that though none of us are perfect, and we may not get it right the first, second, or third time around—we all still have the option to choose what is right over what is wrong.

Acknowledgments

I would like to acknowledge my husband, David, who is my rock and the love of my life, who has stood by me through all the ups and downs and has never left my side. Honey, this journey would not have begun without you. Thank you for everything.

To all my family and friends far and near, particularly my sisters in Alpha Kappa Alpha, thank you for all your words of encouragement and for your continued support. I love you guys more than you could ever know.

To my illustrator, Cynthia, who saw my vision exactly as I did and brought my characters to life, thank you. You're awesome!

To my editor, Hallie—I am forever indebted to you for all of the knowledge you have shared with me.

And finally, to Milli and all the wonderful and patient people at Brown Books Publishing Group, thank you for making my dream become a reality.

I would like to thank Attorney Luckett for endorsing our book and for believing in our projects. Rest In Peace Bill and our condolences to Francine and the Luckett family for their loss.

Attorney Bill Luckett, former Clarksdale mayor and co-owner of Ground Zero Blues Club, died Thursday, October 28, 2021.

Katie lived with her twin, Kimmie, in a big yellow house with a red front door. The twins were eight-and-a-half years old, and they loved each other very much. They looked just alike, but they had different personalities.

Kimmie liked being inside. She liked painting her nails, going shopping with her mom, and anything shiny and glittery.

atie liked being outside. She liked riding her irt bike, playing games with the neighbors, nd wearing shorts and SPORTS JERSEYS.

But at the start of each new week, both girls enjoyed going to church on Sunday. They put on their beautiful dresses, sang in the choir, and listened to Pastor Jimmy talk about Jesus.

"Being right with Christ means loving everyone and treating everyone the same," Pastor Jimmy always said in Sunday school.

"Matthew 22:37-39 says, 'Thou shalt love the Lord thy God with all thy heart, and with all thy soul, and with all thy mind. This is the first and great commandment. And the second is like unto it, Thou shalt love thy neighbor as thyself.'

"Remember that," he told them. "Those are verses to live by." And Pastor Jimmy also told them, "Always tell the truth. Above anything in this world, ALWAYS TELL THE TRUTH."

the law?
37 Je'-sus said unto him, Thou shalt love the Lord thy God with all thy heart, and with all thy soul, and with all thy mind.
38 This is the first and great commandment.
39 And the second is like unto it, Thou shalt love thy neighbour as thyself.
40 On these two commandments hang all the law and the prophets.
11 While the Phar'-i-sees were gathered together

So, Katie knew she was in trouble one day when a horrible accident happened. She was playing baseball with Tim from next door. Tim threw a fastball. Katie swung. She hit.

CRASH!

Katie had hit her ball clean through Mr. and Mrs. Mumford's front kitchen window!

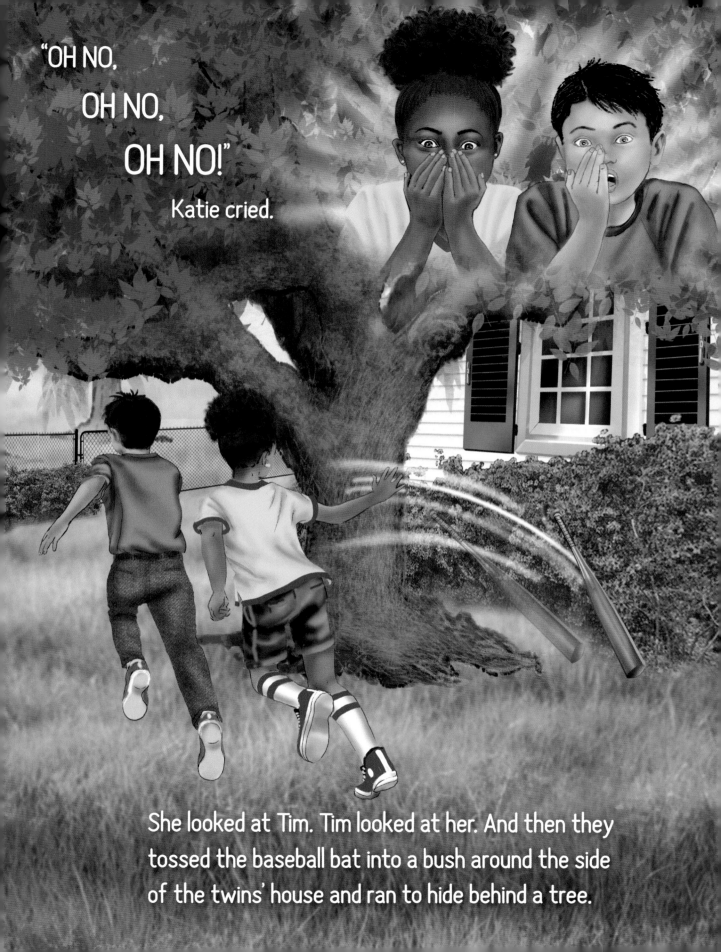

"OH NO,
OH NO,
OH NO!"
Katie cried.

She looked at Tim. Tim looked at her. And then they tossed the baseball bat into a bush around the side of the twins' house and ran to hide behind a tree.

Peeking out from behind the tree, they saw Mr. Mumford come out of his house. They saw him looking all around.

"We're going to be in so much trouble!" Tim said with tears in his eyes.

Katie looked over at her friend. She knew this was all her fault. "You're not in trouble," she told him. "Don't worry. I'll tell Mr. Mumford what happened. After all, I'm the one who hit the ball. Go home, Tim. It'll all be fine."

Tim wasn't sure about leaving, but he listened anyway. He let himself out the backyard gate and went home to his family.

Katie went back to her front yard. "Hey, Katie!" Mr. Mumford called. "Someone busted my front window! Did you see any kids playing baseball out here?"

Mr. Mumford looked **ANGRY.**

Katie looked at the bush where she had hidden her baseball bat.

She felt scared and guilty.

So, she didn't tell the truth. She shook her head.
"I haven't seen anyone," she told him. "I just came
outside when I heard the crash."

Since Katie had never lied to Mr. Mumford before,
he just shook his head. "Alright." He went back inside.

Days passed, and Katie still didn't tell the truth.
She didn't tell her parents or the Mumfords,
even though she'd promised Tim.

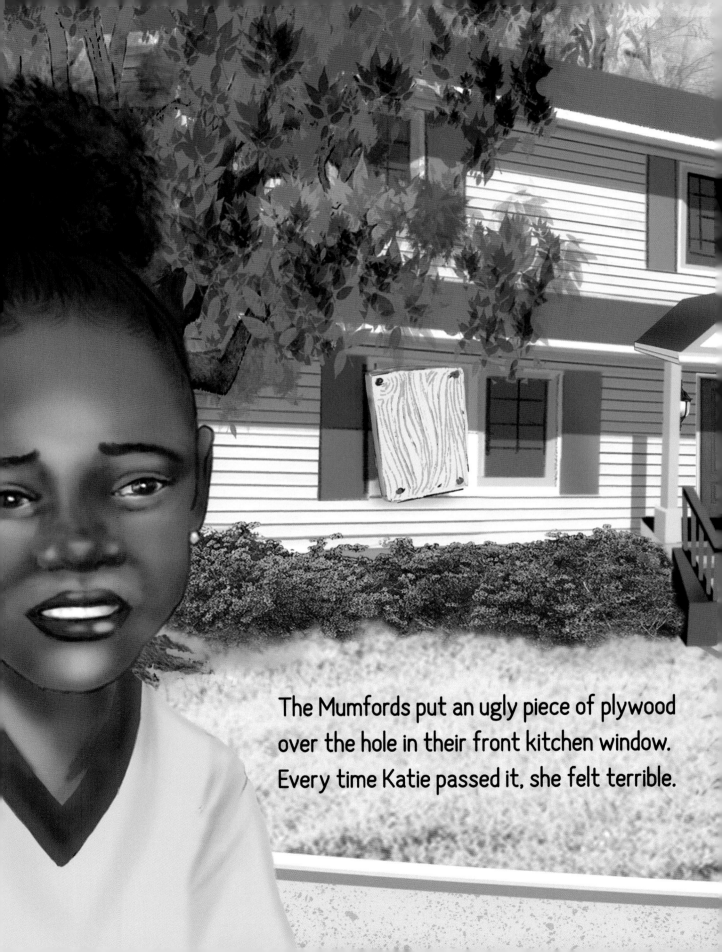

The Mumfords put an ugly piece of plywood over the hole in their front kitchen window. Every time Katie passed it, she felt terrible.

The next Saturday, Katie didn't even want to go outside. She didn't want to ride her dirt bike or play any games with the neighbors. Not if it meant seeing that window. She didn't even want to wear a sports jersey. She stayed inside in her pajamas and watched TV with Kimmie.

"What's wrong?" Kimmie asked after lunch. "You're acting weird today."

Katie told Kimmie what had happened.

"You need to tell Mom and Dad and the Mumfords," Kimmie said. "You won't feel better till you do."

"You didn't see Mr. Mumford's face, Kimmie," Katie said. "He looked so **MAD.**

"Sure, but it's better to tell him," Kimmie answered. "It's the right thing to do. You just ask Pastor Jimmy in Sunday school tomorrow. You know he says to ALWAYS tell the truth."

But Katie didn't ask Pastor Jimmy the next day during Sunday school. Kimmie felt impatient with her twin. She knew Katie was just scared. She wasn't going to tell on her. But there was nothing wrong with giving Katie a little push, she thought.

So, when Pastor Jimmy started telling them about the greatest commandments again, Kimmie raised her hand. "Pastor Jimmy," she said, "when God said love your neighbor as thyself, did God mean love your NEXT-DOOR neighbor as thyself?"

"Well, Kimmie," Pastor Jimmy said, "that's a good question. God wants you to love THE ENTIRE WORLD! Your neighbor can be anyone: your family, your friend, your classmate, your teacher, and yes, your NEXT-DOOR neighbor."

Speak
the
Truth

Matthew 22:37-39

(37) Jesus said unto him, Thou shalt love the Lord thy God with all thy heart, and with all thy soul, and with all thy mind.

(38) This is the first and great commandment.

(39) And the second is like unto it, Thou shalt love thy neighbour as thyself.

"And one way of loving your neighbor is to TELL THEM THE TRUTH, right?" Kimmie asked.

"Right," Pastor Jimmy said. "You should always, always tell the truth."

Katie slumped in her seat. She knew that to truly love God, her family, and her friends, she had to be honest. She wanted to do the right thing.

After church, Katie walked up to her mom and dad, who were talking to Mr. and Mrs. Mumford about their broken window. "I got an estimate on the window," Mr. Mumford said with a sad look on his face, "and it's going to cost $175 to fix!"

Katie started to tear up. Kimmie came up and held her hand. She smiled and nodded at her, and Katie felt a little bit braver. "Excuse me," Katie said. "Mr. and Mrs. Mumford?"

"Yes, sweet girl?" Mrs. Mumford asked.

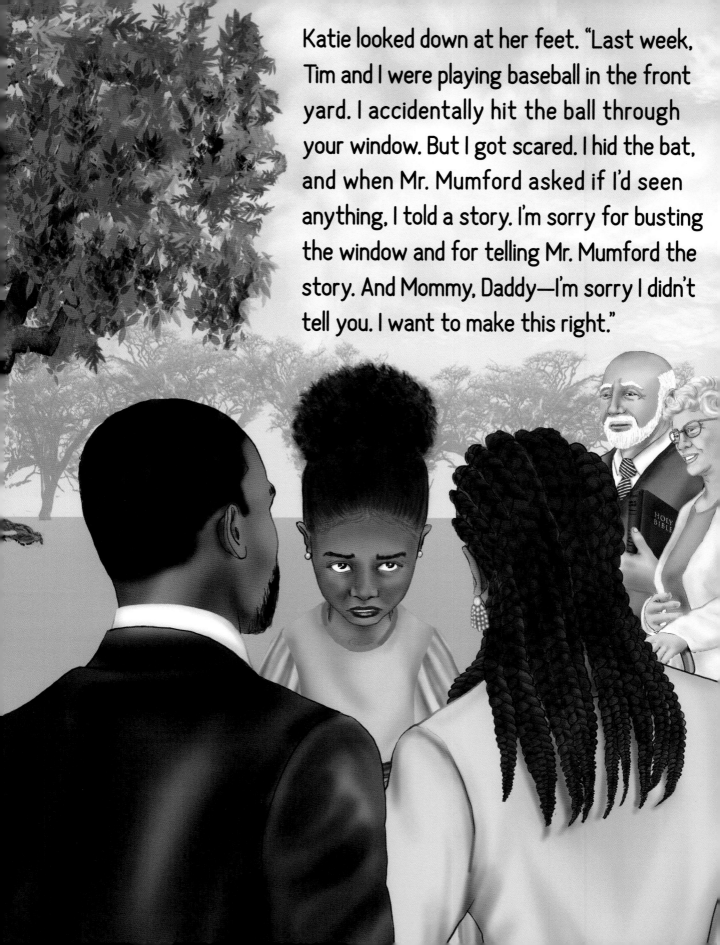

Katie looked down at her feet. "Last week, Tim and I were playing baseball in the front yard. I accidentally hit the ball through your window. But I got scared. I hid the bat, and when Mr. Mumford asked if I'd seen anything, I told a story. I'm sorry for busting the window and for telling Mr. Mumford the story. And Mommy, Daddy—I'm sorry I didn't tell you. I want to make this right."

"Thank you for telling us the truth," Mom said.

Katie's mother arranged for her to spend Saturdays helping Mr. and Mrs. Mumford do chores around their house until the cost of the broken window was paid for.

But even though Katie wouldn't be playing outside for a while, she did feel better. The Mumfords weren't angry with her. They knew she had made a mistake, and they were happy she had taken responsibility for breaking the window.

And when Katie turned back to her sister, Kimmie was smiling. She gave Katie a hug and whispered,

"I'm proud of you. Always tell the truth!"

Note from the Author

I wrote this book with my children and future generations in mind. Girls and boys, my dearest readers, whatever situations you find yourself facing in life, remember that no person, situation, or object is bigger than God. He is always waiting for you to kneel in prayer to talk to Him, and if you confess your sins, He is ready and eager to forgive you and wash away whatever wrong you have done. Like Katie in the story, you will find that so much anxiety will be lifted from your shoulders and that a lot of good things can happen for you if you are honest and ALWAYS TELL THE TRUTH.

Love,
Kyra

About the Author

Kyra Robinson has always loved speaking, writing, and singing to others. Born in Clarksdale, Mississippi, famously known as the "home of the blues," Kyra took her love of music with her to Mississippi Valley State University, where she attended on a music scholarship, danced with the majorettes as a Satin Doll, sang in three different choirs, and minored in voice. She obtained her bachelor of arts in mass communications, and after a follow-up master's degree in public administration and urban studies at the University of Akron in Akron, Ohio, Kyra went on to a career in broadcasting and television, working with News Channel 12 in Jackson, Mississippi, Black Entertainment Television in Washington, DC, and the Black Family Channel and Turner Broadcasting in Atlanta, Georgia.

But when an accident at work left Kyra disabled in 2017, her entire trajectory in life changed. She began to write books and focus on her passion to inspire and teach children with her writing, guiding them toward their God-given purposes in life.

Kyra is a loving wife and mother of three. She enjoys baking and cooking the old Southern dishes her mom taught her, and to this day, when she is not working on her writing, she can often be found in her kitchen, making a joyful noise at the top of her lungs.

About the Illustrator

Cynthia Meadows, a native Texan, has always had a passion for creating her own characters and inspiring the imagination of children with her art. After graduating from Rice University with a BA in architecture, she decorated cakes and painted personal art pieces, eventually venturing into commercial art. Since moving to Dallas, she has illustrated storyboards, finished art for multiple ad agencies, painted pet portraits and murals, done faux finishing, worked with decorative concrete, and illustrated marker comps and storyboards.